A Note to Parents and Teachers

Kids can imagine, kids can laugh and kids can learn to read with this exciting new series of first readers. Each book in the Kids Can Read series has been especially written, illustrated and designed for beginning readers. Humorous, easy-to-read stories, appealing characters, and engaging illustrations make for books that kids will want to read over and over again.

To make selecting a book easy for kids, parents and teachers, the Kids Can Read series offers three levels based on different reading abilities:

Level 1: Kids Can Start to Read

Short stories, simple sentences, easy vocabulary, lots of repetition and visual clues for kids just beginning to read.

Level 2: Kids Can Read with Help

Longer stories, varied sentences, increased vocabulary, some repetition and visual clues for kids who have some reading skills, but may need a little help.

Level 3: Kids Can Read Alone

Longer, more complex stories and sentences, more challenging vocabulary, language play, minimal repetition and visual clues for kids who are reading by themselves.

With the Kids Can Read series, kids can enter a new and exciting world of reading!

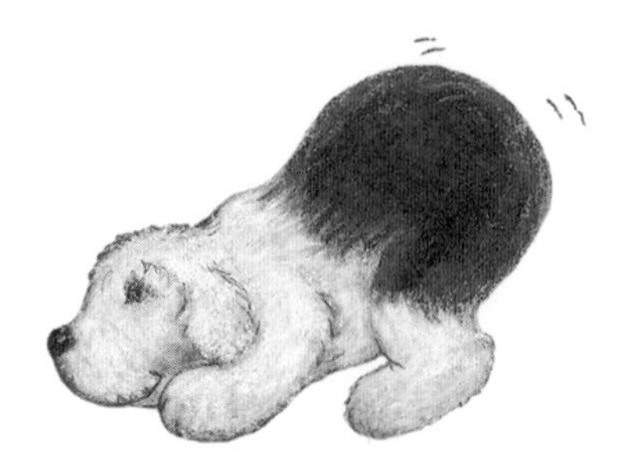

Sam Gets Lost

Written by Mary Labatt

Illustrated by Marisol Sarrazin

Kids Can Press

Kids Can Press acknowledges the financial support of the Ontario Arts Council, the Canada Council for the Arts and the Government of Canada, through the BPIDP, for our publishing activity.

Published in Canada by
Kids Can Press Ltd.
29 Birch Avenue
Toronto, ON M4V 1E2

Published in the U.S. by
Kids Can Press Ltd.
2250 Military Road
Tonawanda, NY 14150

www.kidscanpress.com

Edited by David MacDonald
Designed by Stacie Bowes and Marie Bartholomew
Printed in Hong Kong, China, by Book Art Inc., Toronto

The hardcover edition of this book is smyth sewn casebound.
The paperback edition of this book is limp sewn with a drawn-on cover.

CM 04 0 9 8 7 6 5 4 3 2 1
CM PA 04 0 9 8 7 6 5 4 3 2 1

National Library of Canada Cataloguing in Publication Data

Labatt, Mary, [date]

Sam gets lost / written by Mary Labatt ; illustrated by Marisol Sarrazin.

(Kids Can read)
ISBN 1-55337-562-9 (bound). ISBN 1-55337-563-7 (pbk.)

I. Sarrazin, Marisol, 1965– II. Title. III. Series: Kids Can read (Toronto, Ont.)

PS8573.A135S243 2004 jC813'.54 C2003-902330-3
PZ7

Kids Can Press is a Corus™ Entertainment company

Joan got her car keys.

"Let's go downtown," she said.

"Woof!" said Sam.

"I like car rides," she thought.

Joan and Bob got into the car.

Sam jumped in the back.

The car went fast.

"Yahoo!" thought Sam.

"I like to go fast!"

Joan drove downtown.

She had to stop for a red light.

"This is not good," thought Sam.

"I like to go fast."

Sam saw lots of people.

And she saw bikes and scooters

and strollers and baby buggies.

"Wow!" thought Sam.

"Everyone is having fun!

I need to have fun.

I am getting out."

Sam hopped up on the trunk.

Then she jumped down.

Sam saw lots of feet –

big feet, little feet,

old feet and young feet.

Sam saw lots of wheels –

bicycle wheels, scooter wheels,

stroller wheels and baby buggy wheels.

Sam poked her nose

into a garbage can.

"Get out of the garbage!" said a man.

Sam stuck her nose

into a lady's bag.

"Get out of my bag!" said the lady.

Sam jumped up

to see a baby.

"Don't touch my baby!" said the mother.

Sam sat down.

"This is not fun!" she thought.

"Car rides are better.

I will go back to the car."

Sam looked for Joan's blue car.

She saw lots of blue cars.

But she did not see Joan's car.

Sam looked up the street.

Then she looked down the street.

"Where did Joan and Bob go?"

she thought.

"This is bad," thought Sam.

"Joan and Bob are lost!

I will find them."

Sam looked and looked.

She ran one way.

Then she ran the other way.

Sam bumped into a lady.

The lady dropped her apples.

Apples rolled all over the sidewalk.

Sam jumped over the apples.

"I have to find Joan and Bob,"

she thought.

Sam looked and looked and looked.

Sam bumped into a man.

The man dropped his cans.

Cans rolled all over the sidewalk.

Sam jumped over the cans.

“I have to find Joan and Bob,”

she thought.

Sam looked and looked and looked.

Sam bumped into a boy.

The boy dropped his gumballs.

Gumballs rolled onto the street.

Sam slid on the gumballs.

But she did not stop.

"I have to find Joan and Bob," she thought.

Sam ran into the street.

Horns honked.

People yelled.

"Get out of the way, puppy!" yelled a man.

But Sam kept running.

"Joan and Bob are lost," thought Sam.

"I have to find them!"

Big hands grabbed Sam.

“SAM!” yelled someone.

“What are you doing?”

Sam looked up.

It was Bob!

Joan was there, too!

"Poor Sam," said Joan.

"You were lost."

Sam was surprised.

"I was NOT lost!" she thought.

"YOU were lost!"

"Puppies are NEVER lost!"